Rosie Ray
A Tale of Watery Wings

Suzanne Tate

Illustrated by James Melvin

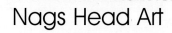

Nags Head Art

To Mary Riddick
who lovingly inspired her students
to follow their dreams

Library of Congress Catalog Card Number 2002096213
ISBN 978-1-878405-40-1
ISBN 1-878405-40-3
Published by
Nags Head Art, Inc., P.O. Box 2149, Manteo, NC 27954
Copyright © 2003 by Nags Head Art, Inc.

Rosie Ray

HAPPY READING!

This book is especially for:

_____

Suzanne Tate,
Author—
brings fun and
facts to us in her
Nature Series.

James Melvin,
Illustrator—
brings joyous life
to Suzanne Tate's
characters.

Suzanne and James in costume

Rosie Ray was soft and smooth —
a newly born ray pup.

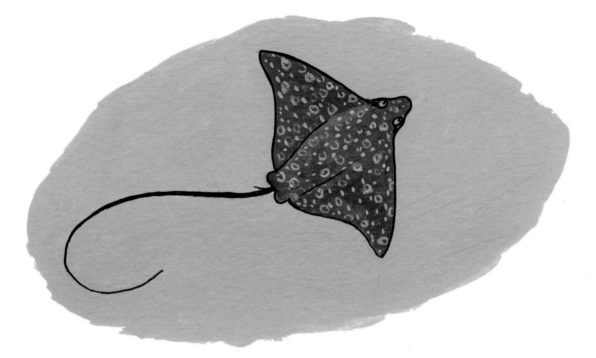

She was a spotted eagle ray,
a strange fish with no bones.
And her wide flat fins were like wings!

Rosie's mother had given birth to four ray pups.
The baby eagle rays had long tails
and lots of spots.

You could say they were
Dalmatians of the deep!

Right away, the eagle ray mother began
to swim away from her pups.
"Wait, Mama," Rosie Ray cried.
"Where are you going?"

"Oh, you don't need me!"
her mother replied.

"You already know how to do everything —
to flap your fins and swim," the ray mother said.
"And how to get food."

"But what if some scary animal
comes near me?" Rosie asked.
"I want you to protect me."

"See that stinging spine on your tail? It will help to protect you from enemies," Rosie's mother replied.

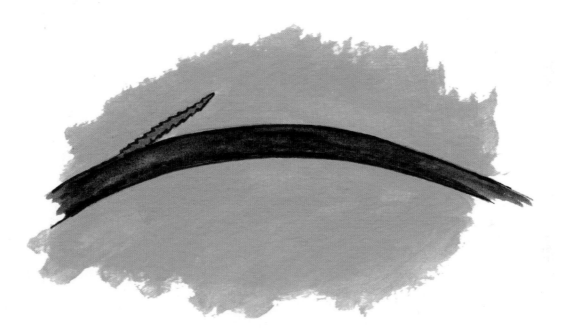

"But you should bury in the seabed if you sense danger," she said as she swam away.

It wasn't long before a dark shape appeared in the water above the eagle ray pups.

Rosie saw it first.
"Quick! Let's flap our fins and bury ourselves," she said.

"Yes!" Ronnie Ray — a brother pup — agreed.
"Our spotted tops will hide us in the sand."
The ray pups quickly fanned their flat fins.

Sand swirled and covered their bodies.

Then, the little ray pups didn't fan a fin.
Only their eyes peeked out!

It was just in time!

That dark shape was a big,
hungry hammerhead shark.

He was a close cousin to rays.
But they were only food to him!

The baby rays knew to stay still until danger swam away.
"I'm hungry! Can we come out now?" Ronnie asked.
"We can look for food," Rosie replied, "if we are careful."

Ronnie began to shove his snout into the sandy seabed.
The snout on his head was shaped like a bird's bill!
He could scoop up little mollusks buried in the sand.

"Come on!" Ronnie called to the others.
"There's plenty of food for us here."

Rosie and the other little ray pups all
shoved their snouts through the sand.
Little fish followed them for scraps.

The young spotted eagle rays needed a lot of food to grow.
But they could smell well and find lots of prey.

Soon, all of the little mollusks
were scooped up and gone!

"I'm going to move to a new place,"
Rosie said. "We will too," said the other ray pups,
flapping their watery wings.

The young rays found lots of food.
They grew stronger and larger.

One day, Rosie and Ronnie swam away from the others.
They "flew" fast with their wide, watery wings.

All of a sudden, Ronnie discovered that he could leap out of the water!

"Watch this!" he called to Rosie.
He flapped his fins and went
up and out of the water!

"I'm going to try that too!" Rosie said.
She fanned her fins fast and
leaped from the water.

"How graceful you look!" Ronnie exclaimed.

The young eagle rays were having so much fun!
But they forgot to watch for danger.

Big dolphins began to swim in a circle
around the young rays.

Suddenly, they began to toss
Rosie and Ronnie into the air!

The dolphins were having a lot of fun —
but it wasn't a game the rays liked.

"I'm scared!" Rosie cried. "What are we going to do?"
But Ronnie wasn't any help — he was scared too.
Just then, Ronnie was tossed into the air again.

When he came down,
the water made a big splash!

HELPFUL HUMANS were nearby in a boat.
They saw what was happening!

"Look at those beautiful spotted eagle rays,"
one of the HUMANS said. "They are in trouble.
We need to help them."

Quickly, the HELPFUL HUMANS started their motor.
They ran the boat fast — kicking up waves!

Dolphins love to chase boats!
They stopped playing with the rays
and followed the HUMANS.

Rosie and Ronnie were happy to see the dolphins swim away.

"I'm glad that they are leaving us alone," Rosie sighed happily.

"HELPFUL HUMANS were here
at the right time," Ronnie said.
"And now, let's get out of here!"

The young rays
flapped their watery wings
and swam quickly to the bottom of the sea.

Rosie and Ronnie Ray were safe
at last on the sandy seabed.